THE DESERT DREAMS

To Mom,
6 Aug, 2018
Love,

THE DESERT DREAMS

vengeance of a vanished man

Jeffrey M. Reynolds

The brief quotations that appear herein are from Robinson Jeffers and Edward Abbey, both sadly deceased and lost to us; the others are from Cormac McCarthy and Jim Harrison, both very much alive, more so than most, and lucky for us are still out there creating. Their quotes are used by permission.

The people, places, and events herein depicted are an odd sort of history, and they all know who they really are. We just have to live with that.

"SADM" is a military term used late in the book, and stands for:"Special Atomic Demolition Munitions". These are backpackable nuclear weapons weighing about 40 pounds and available in 0.5, 1.0, and 2.0 kiloton strengths. Once armed, there are about two dozen people on earth who could disarm one without setting it off. Obviously, an incredibly useful weapon if you are into serious terrorism.

Printed 2001
First Edition

Printed on acid-free paper

ISBN 0-9618478-0-8

OTHER BOOKS BY JEFFREY M. REYNOLDS

American Space: The Desert

Gifts From the Planet's Heart: Hot Springs of the West

Introduction

The following story is as true as my voice and choice of words can make it and still insure the anonymity of men to whom I owe my life, such anonymity being their choice, as I should have known. The story repeated as dreams now and then for some years, but increasing frequency, intensity, and detail to those dreams over the last few years have made it clear that it speaks both to my present and my future, whatever that may become. It is powerful enough now to both awaken me and intrude on my waking hours. Having attained the status of a waking dream, I can only yield and attempt to give it the homage it deserves. If these past events have other demands to make on my waking hours, I'm sure they will let me know at their convenience. My convenience, of course, has nothing to do with it.

The time and terrain in the journey that follows are ones known well to me, and not the location of the events that I cause to take place there. Too much of the heart of these events speaks to the spirit of the American Desert for me to weave the words anywhere I didn't know intimately and often. I speak only for myself, but every word attempts to do justice to the spirit of the man and the time and the place that actually contained the small miracle itself. This is their story only. That the actual canyon and man still live unmolested is all the tribute that either wants or needs.

May that which they seek seek also them.

J. M. Reynolds
Yakima, WA
Winter, 1997

I

Events repeat. It is, of course, a miracle. Once again. And again the soft gleam of full moonlight illuminates the walls of a canyon over 300 million years deep. The harder darkness of the living strips of green that line the riverbanks — tamarisk and willow, nearly impenetrable, a rare cottonwood — together all that leafed life that gives the Green River its well-earned name frames the pallor of the silt-laden water that drifts so silently here, mile after mile of stillness, life-giving water in a desert's heart.

Again, I find myself at the top of a 300-foot jump-off staring through the night, down this side canyon to The River a quarter mile away. The pale sandbars that dot the water say summer, or perhaps autumn, but it feels too warm for anything later than September. Halfway up the far wall across The River, I can see the huge, tilted slab of sandstone with its two rows of dinosaur tracks laid across the moonlight, their makers as dead and foreign to the imagination here as the swamp they walked in what is now stone and desert vastness. I am glad to find them that far gone: one less thing to hunt for me. I recall all those tens of thousands of names on walls of shiny black granite in The City far away, but the metaphor is fatally flawed: these tracks in the moonlight were made by living things, while those scratches on black granite were made by the dead. So I unrecall, forget.

No spear or bow and arrow fills my hand, but a rifle. Heavy barrel. Synthetic stock. Twentieth Century, or close enough. It's good to be back. And yes, there on the edge of one sand bar, a raft, two tents, assorted gear. Yes. That night. Day One. I know what comes next.

The rifle fits well: Winchester Model 70, .308 calibre, prone position, sandbag for the barrel support. I lie on dry stone now slightly cool, but I can still feel the day's heat radiating from the canyon walls; so midnight, not predawn darkness. I need not look to know: Remington Match King, 168-grain, boat-tailed hollow points, Moly-coated, 5-shot magazine. One is all I'll need this night. Sighted in months ago, mid-river is 520 yards away. The raft and tent would be only some thirty yards further, but this summer air is warmer, a little less dense, so no compensation should be necessary.........

The shift of moonlight and stars says two hours later, but in the wonder of dreams, it's only a moment or two. Dependable as all real histories, an older man steps out of the tent, sparse silver hair shining in the light. The 20-power Leupold scope makes him recognizable, even from here. Not that I have ever met the man; I have merely lived in and survived events he helped make happen and would not stop. He helped others take three years of my life and too much of my spirit; I am here to take all that's left of his. Maybe if I knew him, I wouldn't be here. Maybe if I knew him well I could actually hate him. No matter: he killed by proxy, and I am one of those proxies. I have not forgotten. I still know my job. If he knew me, he'd wish I didn't.

He looks around at the cliffs, the stars, the river, stretches, and walks to the waters' edge. Fumbling at his shorts, he stands still, coaxing his older prostate into cooperation. It shouldn't be this easy, but it is. Stock still, pausing as men do when urinating, I lay the cross hairs on his face in quarter-profile.

Time now to pretend well. The old mantra repeats itself:

"There is no Fear, for I am become Death
No history, no future: I am only Death
No cruelty, no mercy: I am only Death
I have never been anything but Death"

and now is all the time there is..........

Whatever curiosity brings you here, what you hunt for here hunts also you. Welcome to my canyon. This is for all the wasted friends. Breathe. Reelaax. Cross hairs steady. At this distance, the shot will be dead on or short; and if it's short, it becomes a neck or chest shot: both equally fatal at this range. Dead is dead. Aaaim. Whose dream is this that this is so easy? Who wrote this story so well that my target stands alone, offered to me this night? Squeeeee........

Sharp, sudden recoil a wonderful surprise. Magic!

At 2,800 feet per second, the bullet will take over one half second to reach him: time enough to see the muzzle flash, out here in the night, perhaps enough time to turn towards it, curious, the last light he sees. The rolling thunder of the shot, the decrescendo up and down the canyon, the shattered silence wakes me every time........

II

Wide awake very quickly, very still, listening.......No rolling thunder, no echoes. No sound at all. Soft, greyish dawn light at the entrance barely illuminates smooth, nearly detailless sandstone over my head. My eyes struggle with focus a little while — thinking infinity, remembering six to eight feet, finally deciding, seeing the grains of what once was only sand, now rock for thousands of millennia, also now, soon to be sand again, as the endless cycle of erosion and sedimentation continues, inexorable as the River a mile from here. I should be so patient.

So. Not a dream after all, but recent history. Unless, of course, I am someone else's wonderfully detailed, full color dream. Whatever. An action pondered for years, plotted for months, now successfully executed. The simple fact of the occurrence itself energizes my every morning, and this one is no exception. If this is someone else's dream, I like it. A lot. Dream on. I no longer have responsibilities, duties; instead I have memories. The power of so simple a joy is a wonderful elixir, a gentle spice for the secret that is mine alone — if I am patient enough to keep waiting.

A glance at the cave wall to my left to count my neat scratches there: twenty-six. So now day twenty-seven begins. It seems so much longer — it is hard to be still, still only part of the stone, the cliffs, the sidewalls of this small canyon way too close to the murder of Someone Important. It will still be hard weeks from now, but stillness, waiting motionless — the core ethics of survival in the desert — speak to me of the power of mystery. If I am caught, it is only an assassination: but I am not "hashisheen"; have never used that drug; have never even been to the Middle East, yet reasonable, logical explanations will surely follow, myself merely yet another crazed veteran, just another gun nut. No one will wonder much why I have only this one gun. Another week's feeding frenzy for the media, but I will bore them quickly — simple morals that even the Old Testament knew about are not really news, certainly not for long. No. I love my freedom too much, want to keep it too badly, want the mystery of simple revenge to escape the speculations of even the most thoughtful news analyst. But they sure as hell know it wasn't some hunting accident.

I have become now that which I dreamed, and wish to remain thus: the still and peregrine paladin of last seconds, no longer guardian, more wandering yet to come, those last seconds now accomplished. Nothing changes that.

Almost four weeks now! Jesus! I may actually get away with this!

Not if you're stupid enough to celebrate now! Not if you think with adrenaline in your veins. Think about stone. Out of/from stillness:"ex stasis": ecstasy — stillness of stone should suffice. Think about how much water you have left. Think about if they found your inflatable and you have to walk out of here.

Good point: I could escape all those legal powers of the government, and The Desert would not be impressed, not even a little. It would not hesitate to kill me if I am careless or stupid. I am meat out here: I can continue to drink and eat, or I can become food for animals better at it than I am. Freedom has a price. Survival is just a skill.

A few stretching exercises under my light blanket, insulation barely needed in high desert summer. Too many complaining joints and muscles: fifty is too old for this. As if anyone really younger would understand what I was angry about, why I bothered, why I risked my life and freedom for a revenge that may not even be public knowledge. The Former Secretary of Defense (and only formerly alive, I am pleased to add) probably died an accidental death as far as the newspapers know. How tragic. A quiet vacation in beautiful Southern Utah sadly interrupted. I wonder how they convinced the Garfield County Coroner that a 7.62mm hole in the face and no back of the head at all wasn't an extraordinary occurrence in a National Park? Who knows? Plenty of time to find out later, should I survive this little exile. I can only hope that I can maintain muscle tone for two months without ever really leaving this cave.

I look out the small entrance down to the wash bottom below. Two huge, glorious white blossoms decorate the local Jimson Weed bush, still celebrating last week's thunderstorm by investing some hard-earned moisture in reproductive effort. The blossoms will wither by noon. Hopefully the moths or the bats did their job last night and donated a little pollen to the cause while gathering precious moisture and sugar for themselves. I will be here long enough to find out, to see the seed pods form to replace the withered brown ruins of the flower that bloomed once, and died in less than a day.

Ah yes, Loco Weed: contains high levels of strychnine, a stimulant neurotoxin. Any animal stupid enough to devour those inviting, fat, moist leaves will die horribly in sustained epileptic seizures causing respiratory arrest. Also known as Sacred Datura, since Man is stupid enough to call a "religious experience" the chaotic visual hallucinations you get if you can manage to take only a sub-lethal dose of its root. Of course, a little too much (and nobody knows how much that is, since the strychnine content of the root of any one plant varies from year to year, depending on weather, nutrients, luck, etc.) and you get all these "visions" just before it kills you. Surely we can do better.

Maybe not.

Nevertheless, I should continue to take inspiration from the plant: all that effort, all that risk of life-giving water to desert air (although wisely minimized by blooming only at night) to maybe, only very much maybe, go on a little longer, a part of you somewhere else, perhaps a little safer, a little richer than here.

Then again, I can always depress myself, thinking how many of my fellow citizens would still be alive if I had killed a Then Secretary of Defense 30 years ago, instead of only a Former Secretary of Defense now, now that all those thousands have been dead twenty-five years. But I was not alive then to do it: the Young Man then who became me now neither knew nor cared enough to guess what would become of his innocence, his naive patriotism, thanks to the efforts and lack of courage of men he was foolish enough to trust and sufficiently ignorant to follow. But I am alive now, even more alive than I have been in decades, because one man foolish enough to admit his mistake in public twenty-five years too late to do any good did not live long to enjoy his guilt or obtain forgiveness.

I had almost forgotten when I heard of his admission. There was no way I could forgive it. Vengeance has given me one very specific dream, but it has given me also better and more energizing sleep than I have known for far too long.

4

I wish others besides myself a little more gentler sleep, a slightly quieter rest, knowing that payback time can come even for the High and Important. It is a Waking Dream I wish for others, comrades-in-arms long forgotten, barely rememberable.

It is an unforeseen pleasure to be a pest to the bureaucracy I once served with lethal efficiency, and now have similarly opposed. I will remain a pest, however tiny, only if I am not found. So I shall not be found: the briefness of life demands a few compensatory pleasures.

A good long drink of water from one of my 20-liter water bladders. I am back up to ten full bladders after venturing out during last week's rain and minor flash flood to restock. It was good to get out and get a 360-degree view of the desert after three weeks in the cave. Even if they want me bad enough to use satellite technology, I figured I was safe under the storm. Obviously, I guessed right. I am probably way too paranoid: the government had used his skills for decades and he was long retired, so I doubt they care enough to make a full effort, although the noise and activity level of the first three days convinced me somebody was at least briefly pissed.

Sorry guys; it's going to take your best to get me because I've been trained by your best, long ago, and I have not forgotten patience and I'm not going to make a mistake. I am not proud enough of this to brag to anyone, not ever, so the secret is mine alone. Guess all you want at who and why. If I'm lucky, a few people in power will lose a minute's sleep or two wondering who's next, never guessing the answer is no one. May the guilty lie sleepless though no one hunts them.

Maybe no one hunts for me.

I'll wait anyway: it's not a learning experience if you don't live through it. Besides, I wouldn't want my teammates long past to think they wasted their time training some impetuous idiot.

It's not as if I don't have the time to do it right. Mary died three years ago, and after twenty-one years together, I doubt anyone will fill a hole in my life that big, even if I live enough years to make it possible. Way too big a hole. The thought of what my future lacks because of her absence brings an aching, heart-felt pain even now. If she were still alive, I'd be here hiking in late summer high desert with her just for the simple wonder and daily gifts of surprise that this impossibly sculpted space seems to offer unbidden to anyone who really takes the time to wander here, and makes the effort to carry enough water to survive the heat. Instead, a brief admission by a stranger from a war long gone ignites a fire hot enough to kill him years later, only because I was free and purposeless enough to care to take vengeance for crimes long accomplished, a war long over and lost.

Idle hands are retribution's playground. And he was stupid enough to go public with a vacation plan, a vacation in one of my playgrounds, frequently visited for 30 years, far better known to me than to USGS maps, most Park Rangers, and certainly anyone he cared to bring with him. And now, obviously, better known to me than to anyone they cared to send out to hunt for me. Plenty of good luck for me this year. But now I am only here to hide, having killed, all the reasons, theirs and mine, equally meaningless.

I do hate spending this much time in a space I love, but not being able to wander freely. I know a dozen places nearby that offer spectacular views for sunrise, and after over four weeks here, I've not seen a one. Every sunset, every storm cloud, moonrise, moonset — too much going on without me, too much way more important than my individual survival; except, of course, to me. Such selfishness serves me well right now; I might as well appreciate it.

But it is hard, after so many visits to the desert, to take life too seriously. It took me years of sweat and solitude out here to finally stop seeing this desert as a space of metaphors, to finally abandon the anthropomorphic thoughts I brought with me, visit after visit, that while they comforted me, only served to ground my psyche on a foundation built far away, a home base that has no meaning here, and never did, however much I may wish otherwise.

I no longer wish otherwise. This is the ultimate freedom: accepting this space for what it actually is, and adapting my wants and needs to what it actually offers, knowing forever in my heart that I can offer it nothing as long as I live. Dead, of course, my body can be of use here. Someday, that would not be a bad destiny; perhaps only fair (even fairness a foreign concept to all this rock and sky, even to the coyote far away, howling her barely audible welcome to this day).

I want to once again enter the life of this vast desert, be it, and the life of the ancient peaks at its edge — the Henrys, the Abajos, the La Sals — the patience of stone, the careful, timeless, ceaseless whittling of water and wind, the inescapable killing oddness of cold and snow in high desert winter. I want to disremember the men who act like gods, the humans who can only dream gods like themselves, civilizations that can see only themselves as the purpose of the universe, who may admit intellectually to a time before men but never know it emotionally, in their hearts where they really believe. And whole cultures incapable of imagining any end at all, or if there is any imaginable end, they or their children will be there to see it.

I think not.

But there are not words for it, words for telling about time like stars, boiling in the nights, each pinpoint blinding plasmic scream in the dark knowing more about hours and ages than I can imagine. To go beyond hours and ages, be all things at all times, all these returns and passages spiralling into a motionless and timeless center, centuries like hills on the horizon, any year at all as visible as any other, all there simultaneously to be walked in, seen, experienced......

It is impossible to express the excellence I have found there, the pure clarity of thought, vision, purpose that is only itself, relates to no other, no murmur of memory, no distraction, only itself, no time but perfectly spherical eternity............

All this silence needs no defense: impossibly sculpted, rigid, delightfully and magically echoic, infinitely patient silence resides here, awaits only wind or coyote or the very rare rifle shot for erasure. Only to return, powerfully dependable, probably tomorrow. Gravity alone leans on the land: 4,000 miles of remorseless rock casually reflects 100 miles of air, uncounted parsecs of night sky. Pale and motionless, this living interface pauses, the true and honest face of the earth; not a mother's, nor a father's, lovely and terrible, irrevocably inhuman, the lone visible bridge between stone and wind, earth and air, geologic eras and mortal minutes.

No dream suffices. Imagination, however potent, is utterly unequal to this space. The magic the world possesses less of every year is here a daily presence. No memory recalls such simple purposeless stillness; no human mind values meaninglessness higher than itself; I know of none who labor in the dark for the ultimate attainment of effortless insignificance. The silence that awaits us, will become us, is an unwelcomed fate for our human psyche. Forebodingly empty, forbiddingly timeless, it is our loathed but dependable destiny, coming regardless to take us by force. But we want to choose.

Actually, we did choose. All our self-sacrificing constituent cells, countless myriad molecules, would rather be conscious — however briefly, whatever the price. We wish to see the stars, smell flowers, taste blood, touch another, hear the music of the spheres — now and then, here and there — when we could so easily still be blind and lifeless atoms of all this beauty that surrounds us.

All this silence, however huge and comfortingly eternal, was not enough. And we chose. We still do: dying is so easy, but nothing seems more precious to us than right now.

III

One hour of hard exercise, mostly working the legs, now while the morning coolness persists. Even so, I work up a good sweat, wasting water because I have plenty. I know this country too well, know that the simple, near-total aridity of the air itself can suck a gallon a day out of you, effortlessly, and by the time your thirst catches up to the loss, the bounce in your step is long gone and you wonder why you feel so tired. And I cannot afford to be either out of shape or a little dry when the time comes to walk out of here.

Water makes all the difference. Even the small window of my cave shows the fantastic, indescribable beauty of the unimaginable rock forms all around: towers on the skyline, colors and textures in the canyon walls, strange little hollows carved into the centuries, all of them altering, minute to minute, as the sun moves, and the daily play of light and shadow dances through the rocks. A day without water here and there is only thirst, too many miles of god-forsaken stone, the killing heat of desert daylight. Water is the magic. Erosive forces of water sculpted it to strange beauty, made it all wonderful, awesome, and with just enough water inside you, your mind can see it, sing its praises, rejoice in the visions spread out before you.

The balance is very fine, and anyone who loves this land, wanders in it long or well or often, hasn't at one time cursed its uncaring nature, lethal heat, debilitating aridity, inhuman vastness. Even though, between efforts to find just the right words to curse it effectively, you know you are here by your own very conscious choice and efforts, and that if you live, you will be here again. It is simply just that wonderful, and just that terrible.

So journey after journey here in the relative dampness of Spring, lugging empty water bladders in my pack and filling them at the seep down-canyon, getting ready for the long wait of summer. Food, too, of course — no need to lose too much weight. 2,500 calories a day and 60 days worth packed in and stored, now about half gone. I took different routes each hike in, but the canyons force certain repetitions, so I used the wash bottoms and hoped for rain. And got it several times in the two weeks I labored to stock this place, scout out the river, sight in the rifle.

I always wondered what others thought of scattered rifle fire over a few days out here, knowing the sound would carry for miles. But few were here to hear it. I only saw three groups floating the River go by in late March, and only one came up to the base of the jump-off, and they seemed ignorant of the route to get above it.

That has been the history here the last ten years or so: More and more people are floating the River, but fewer and fewer of them know much about the side canyons, and few seem to do much random exploring far from the River. Just as well: it remains easy, even in the height of tourist season to get away, be alone, see desert only. And I have been just here for over a month, and except for the three days after the shooting, no one has walked this side canyon. Major side canyon, too: the USGS maps even have a name for it, and the contours are even helpful, except at the jump-off, of course. Nothing like a 300 foot vertical surprise to rim you up, slow you down. Actually, stop you cold from below, unless you are very curious, but from above the route around is surprisingly apparent and remarkably easy, considering the drop itself.

Shucks, considering all the chopper noise I heard those three days, I'll bet every man and dog that walked this canyon came in by helicopter. Hard to surprise anyone out here with one of those: even at full speed, you hear them five minutes before they show up. And what you see from above — all those ridiculous forms and absurd colors — is so distracting, you're lucky if you don't fly into something huge, rigid, and fatal, much less spot some fragment of evidence that might suggest a place to start searching. Ah well, they failed to find me, and that's all that matters. To me.

But I have been lucky. A wet Spring erased all evidence of my comings and goings only days after I left. And four months later, I climbed up-canyon to find food, water, sewage container, and rifle right where I left them, undisturbed. And the nagging question of whether a precision instrument would remain exactly as I left it after four months had been answered when the only shot I took in those four months went right where the scope said it would. The rest is merely patience.

I ponder a moment a small side canyon one canyon system south of here. A small crack in the rock off what is called Shot Canyon, its geology is out of place here. A small pocket of much softer and more darkly pigmented sedimentary rock, it has eroded almost magically into a highly convoluted, complex, seemingly organic crevasse of dark stone interrupted here and there by   fossilized shells — some pale distant relative of the Chambered Nautilus — shining in a narrow space so magical, so foreign to the ocean they swam some 200 million years ago, that no label for the space could do it justice, or even hint at its wonder to the minds of mere mortals like myself. To sit in there for a day, and watch the high sun of summer reflect, re-reflect off the higher walls above, a glow with a living lustre, first here, then there, now over there, sometimes mere seconds between radical alterations in the vision, it pulses with light. If there really is a heart of the desert, I have thought since the first day I saw this that it beats here, every day the sun shines.

The search here in the desert has always been for an inexplicably suitable location — indescribable beforehand, but instantly recognizable at first meeting — a space for the ongoing celebration of simple surprise. Discovery of such solves no problems, except where to go anytime you have a spare day, but it will always be forever an omen of good fortune, some kind of built in denial to an otherwise merciless natural world; perhaps an active wish for the worth of us all. It my be all that really matters here.

It is an astonishing experience, every time. It is there, now and then, that I have been able to lose the thread of self, to let go of the right end and drift out a little further, a precious little. And it is out there, finally a little bit adrift, ungrounded, that I have been able to merge the mind's total experience and heartbreaking brevity into a single, graspable, explicable unit — a lone memory for the planet's self.

While the little canyon remains unnamed, and properly so, I still reflexively label it every time I think about it: Occasional Canyon. I mean, it's always a true canyon, but I've only been able to find it about half the times I try to go there. And its not like Shot Canyon is some huge, extensive maze; it's not. Not having had problems like this elsewhere, I've simply decided that the canyon is only occasionally there. I've just been very fortunate that it has been there half the times I've looked for it. For all I know, that will change; has already changed. For all I know, that little canyon is gone now, never to return, and no matter how often in the future I seek for it, I have seen it for the last time. It may, in fact, consciously decide to never return. Fossilized shells can swim their sea of stone without the likes of me.

Can there be for those stones, as for me, moments of faith, instants when being and believing are absolutely identical?

I have, of course, no recorded data. And nothing to prove.

Memories like that are more than sufficient of the absolute and marvelous for my mortal self.

Yet still I plotted revenge and murder, worked hard at it, did it well, all the while knowing, really knowing in my heart that there was nothing to prove. Nothing provable with it worth knowing.

And still, now four weeks later, it feels wonderful.

There is no pleasure in the memory of the killing; only, at last, a single period at the end of a sentence written largely in blood decades ago, a sentence written by my target and the government he helped create. And written, also, by myself and my comrades in arms — we who gave the blood willingly, believed in the history and the symbols of the nation we were born to, and so, tragically, believed in the government itself. That government, our government, stood behind those symbols, used them for armor, and debased them, forever devalued the memory of all those who died so long ago to bring me the irreplaceable luck of the place of my birth. The now inescapable curse.

Knowing now the belief was misplaced is merely knowledge, facts only. Such knowledge is not power; it is not even close to wisdom. But my simple vengeance is freedom: freedom to believe again, should I find them worthy. I alone am the judge.

Still human. I can tell.

There is no real risk, no way of ever becoming lost, when the whereabouts of everything else has no importance, takes on its true significance for awhile. The truly precious friends, the few who hold me irreplaceably dear, are all dead now. I alone am the fire that remembers. Here, in me, we are not parted. My dreams are now their dreams; my memories all that remain of them. Here, where I am, is enough.

Still, anticipating my long wait, I brought books. Only a few, and in the way of the age-old "desert island" question, I thought they would be difficult choices, but it was surprisingly easy. There really are very few strangers you want to listen to again and again. Entertainment is a brief confection; literature is a prolonged, perhaps lifelong pleasure. I look forward, even now, to choosing the day's author to pass the noonday heat.

Edward Abbey's DESERT SOLITAIRE was an easy choice, most of it written 40 miles from here (as the crow flies, not as the crow packs a rucksack, not in this rock garden). Robinson Jeffers' SELECTED POETRY was another easy choice: he has spoken long and well too many times to my spirit for me to dwell in the wild at any length without thinking of him and his power of language.

I should ever be that good. Only in my dreams. And all that strangely lovely sacred violence, purifying vengeance shining through the letters, each word an honorific for a living passion. I still regret finding his poetry for the first time a year after he died: he would have definitely been worth a pilgrimage.

From the living, I chose Cormac McCarthy's THE CROSSING and Jim Harrison's DALVA. The power of language and the message of endurance, honor to one's chosen self, humility before the strength of natural things that pervade both works would be welcome company in a vast and empty desert. Both have been worthy shields against loneliness, self-pity, pride — all those petty emotional responses so unequal, so detrimental to anything done well. And I wish to do this well.

Only in retrospect, only in the long days of introspection after the killing, did I notice that none of the authors were women. Being a man myself, I guess it's reasonable that my kindred spirits would be men also, but that's too easy an explanation. Besides, Harrison's Dalva and Jeffers' California, the woman in"Roan Stallion", and Clare Walker of"The Loving Shepherdess", are three of the most powerful images of women that I carry in my mind. In the way of great words linked well, these imaginary women are more real than most women I've met. Truth is, I've only known three other women that well, and I married two of them. And they went away. So six women to keep my mind company, comment on my meanderings into foolishness, civilize my visions in the dark. Thanks to them all, life goes on. Nothing else does it better.

They loved the earth, but could not stay. Reasons enough to do things well.

"If a man's imagination were not so weak, so easily tired, his capacity for wonder not so limited, he would abandon forever his dreams of the supernatural. He could learn to perceive in water, leaves and silence more than sufficient of the absolute and marvelous, more than enough to console him for the loss of the ancient dreams."

Thanks Ed. I've needed that enough times lately to know it by heart, and it has served me well. Perspective is always valuable when I start taking myself too seriously. And I do.

The odd liquidity of sandstone in this stillness, turquoise for sky, desert air like silk — cool, dry, sensuous, the joy of its touch life-enhancing beyond description. Traces of sage engraved on the air, promising life. The light and the heat one and the same, irreducible. Summer noon, and all things out here that are not stone become light only. The whole metaphoric for nothing at all, itself alone, more than sufficient of the absolute and marvelous.

However mysterious it all occasionally seems, there is no real paradox within these peculiarly beautiful juxtapositions: small living green gestures surrounded by huge breathtaking leaps of stone riddled with evidence of lives past, long dead, silent beyond all need to speak or answer. As they are, so shall we be: fossils, merely memory, only stones.

This beauty really is everywhere here, but mute, spare, vast; life is everywhere, too, but scattered, scarce, stunted, and must be so to endure here. Such enduring stillness attracts powerfully, while its specifics are so tantalizingly elusive, endlessly suggestive of things wordlessly anthropomorphic, perfectly coincident with the eternally inhuman.

Ultimately, eventually, there is only the need to go away, escape to some cool, green, comfortably foreign dampness; there to finally, perhaps, remember all you saw and felt, perceive their infinitely interrelated complexities of gravity and light and time so intimately coexistent here, maybe even understand some truth of what is actually here in the desert, now that you are here no longer, yet forever thankful for its continued existence, somewhere else, somewhere not yours.

You will go back, of course, knowing there is more. There always is.

The day's final glow on hundreds of feet of naked, unencumbered stone bespeaks the reality of this place. Here the green of life, so striking in its contrasts with the slickrock, is just another tool: like water, like wind and weather. All these things are here, each in its own unique ways, only to shape the core, the one pure essence of the spaces. The spirit of the rocks is the truly elemental living form here, the dominant force, the vision, the uniqueness.

The grace.

The bats take to the dusk skies. I still think they seem out of place out here, out in all that space and vastness, even though I've seen them every summer's night I've spent out here in Utah's finest places.

The nearest planets and first stars light the sky. Another day wanders quietly into history. The rifle hanging on the cave wall gathers another day's worth of dust. I cleaned it very well after that one shot; no fingerprints grace its surfaces. I hope to never fire it again: there is something akin to the great Japanese concept of shibumi in never diluting the great and simple purpose of its last shot with anything more mundane. It did what it was built for so well, so effortlessly, that any other purpose seems a lessening, a diminishing of the purity of the moment. Bushido, yet another Japanese code,"the way of the warrior", rich with rules like integrity, justice, courage, contempt of death, goodwill, politeness, sincerity, honor, loyalty, self-control...... probably forgotten, certainly mostly ignored these days, would understand it well. Stainless steel, it will long outlive me here, no doubt a fascinating artifact some year in the future, should the sufficiently curious or lost ever stick their heads in this little hole. But please, not for another couple of months: I want to live. And so do they.

IV

"He squatted over the cougar and touched her fur. He touched the cold and perfect teeth. The eye turned to the moon gave back no light and he closed it with his thumb and sat by her and put his hand upon her bloodied forehead and closed his own eyes that he could see her running in the mountains, running in the starlight where the grass was wet and the sun's coming as yet had not undone the rich matrix of creatures passed in the night before her. Deer and hare and dove and groundvole all richly empaneled on the air for her delight, all nations of the possible world ordained by God of which she was one among and not separate from. Where she ran the cries of the coyotes clapped shut as if a door had closed upon them and all was fear and marvel. He took up her stiff head out of the leaves and held it or he reached to hold what cannot be held, what already ran among the mountains at once terrible and of great beauty, like flowers that feed on flesh. What blood and bone are made of but can themselves not make on any altar nor by any wound of war. What we may well believe has power to cut and shape and hollow out the dark form of the world surely if wind can, if rain can. But which cannot be held never be held and is no flower but is swift and a huntress and the wind itself is in terror of it and the world cannot lose it."

Once again I substitute cougar for the wolf in McCarthy's poetic words of power, here in a moonlit desert where I have seen the cougar, but wolf here is myth for my lifetime, the last native wolf in Southern Utah killed long before I was born. I hope it is true "the world cannot lose it" for I find the power of the world lessened enough in most places. I am merely fortunate to have seen some of the spaces where the power of the world wanders undiluted, rages at whim, unstoppable, gestures magnificently in the casual, seemingly effortless way that bespeaks great skill and unimaginable energy in perfect control. And I am fortunate to reside even now in a small island of untrammeled desert that glows with such powers, gestures of stone and light that I am envious to emulate.

Full moonlight out my little window of an entrance. The wee hours of day 29 now, so of course, dependable as sunrise, it is full moon once again, just like that well-remembered night I shall forever recall only as day 1 — the day I made my life different in inescapable ways with one brief gesture in the dark, down by The River, a mile off in the night.

I wonder if I ever held Mary with such reverence as the cougar was held. Did the images I created with my eyes closed ever praise her comings and goings, what she added to the spaces around her, quite so well? I doubt it. The visions of power were always the selfish ones, the ones that pondered the pain and grief and loss of my life without her. My too-human desire for us to be one person, one entity so much greater than our two parts, that longed-for oneness now forever unattainable, that's the aurorae that flicker in the skies over every vision, every memory, my egocentric universe still unequal to desert stone, desert water, the eye of the cougar.

Even in daytime, I find myself replaying that night of the dreams, the one that became the first scratch on my wall, the one night that so neatly defined before and after. Unlike the dreams, I amuse myself with the immediate aftermath, the echo of my thunder still fading as I resist the temptation to reacquire a sight picture, head bowed, relaxing in the knowledge of a shot done well, killing the curiosity, the need to really know. The tingle at my right shoulder and cheek, reminders of recoil, the rolling thunder of echoes fading into well-earned oblivion, the starkly accentuated silence of the night now returning.

I always wondered what the voice of an old and unspeakable horror would sound like, what music it would most resemble, what words would it use for identity. It's really nice to know at last, however many years too late: the fading echoes, so surprisingly more soprano than true thunder, is my sound now for a healing wound. A horror endured at the cost of some essential aspect of my humanity, now audible, spoken once only to this one long night, a few words decipherable only by myself - the only one who spoke them, the only one here who heard.

Reacquiring through the sight, back in real time again, I see my few words have awakened his companions, both now out of their tents, their faces blurring briefly as they scan up and down river, still trying to understand what they heard, what they see. One even has a handgun, in clear violation of National Park regulations. Tsk, tsk. I am pleased to think my target was still scared enough after all these years to have a bodyguard. I like to think he had almost enough time to really be afraid as the bullet struck. I am pleased to see him so still and horizontal in the moonlight.

They checked the body quickly. The round I'd fired was still supersonic at target, so half his head was gone. Didn't take much to know he was dead. They seemed to hesitate then, no doubt wondering if they, too, were targets. If they were, they'd already be dead. They were jumpy, lots of pointless gestures made too quickly, adrenaline pumping, but seemed to figure some similar conclusion for themselves. One got out a cellular phone. City boy! Ain't no relay tower to talk to out here, dummy!

I backed away from the lip of the jump-off slowly, wishing the two down below a long and sleepless night, staying on the rock, and barefooted it over the slickrock to the back route to my cave, a fine spray of Clorox and a few other chemicals here and there to insure no trace of odor once the sun got to it, but in fine paranoid fashion wandered circuitously back anyway. Not much fear of being seen: no one to see me back in the canyons here, and my skin and the sandstone match colors pretty well. I had contemplated, out of habit from long ago, the shadowy warpaint of camouflage — a little makeup so to help me lose myself — but that was jungle, a place of shadows, and this is desert, a space of light, so what do I know of blending here? Hiding will do. No tracks in the wash bottom, nothing at all up here to tell I was here. Or any human at all, for that matter. Only the most outrageous luck would yield the cave's entrance, the rock all around it so oddly pockmarked by erosion that there is no hint that this one hole keeps going, opens up inside. It was actually 36 hours before anyone thought to walk this side canyon, and they were not that good, not so lucky.

Months ago, I had promised myself and my ghosts of comrades long dead one good shot for all that past and its odd agonies took from us. And now, unlike so many others, I've had my shot. How good was it, really? My blood, warm and effervescent like fine champagne, sings in my veins, erases decades, heals with its every touch. The night is very good.

Ah yes, we whose ideals are oddly retrogressed, still demanding sacrifice, the price of blood actually needed to create worth, render anything at all worthy of our attention, the only cost we truly remember. Even all of Christianity meaningless without the Cross, without the cold steel of nails, the bloody thorns, the slow painful death; ever needing ritual cannibalism — the blood, the body of the Savior — drunk for power, eaten for power, unable to trust our own true humanity as sufficient for any task, our too true mortality somehow a great wall between us and the future, wishing our precious blood offered freely could make a difference, instead of the much harder discipline of days, years, centuries of effort giving even failure its strange indescribable beauty.

I slept not at all that first night, the adrenaline rush kept replaying, the complex task now seemingly so easily accomplished. Then, of course, I compensated by sleeping all morning, waking only in the heat of the afternoon to the sound of helicopters in the distance, no doubt busy harassing every back country jeeper, convinced the assassin would run, had run.

The next day or two, whoever was in charge got more thorough, at least locally. It didn't help. Or I wouldn't be here to wrestle with the words to make it real again.

Miscellaneous daydreaming to supplement the nights, flesh out the details of the night I'd worked so long and hard to make real. Real was very good indeed. Well worth the remembering.

V

My friend from Asia has powers and magic:
He plucks a brown leaf from the cottonwood and gazing upon it,
   gathering and quieting the god in his mind,
Creates a desert more real than the desert, the rock, the actual
appalling presence, the power of the light.
He believes that nothing is real except as we make it.
I, humbler, have found in my blood bred west of the Caucasus,
   a harder mysticism:
Multitudes stand in my mind, but I believe the desert in the bone vault
Is only the bone vault's desert.
Out here is The Desert.
The sun is the light, the cliff is the rock, come shocks and flashes of reality.
The mind passes, the eye closes, spirit itself is a passage;
The beauty of things was born before eyes and sufficient to itself;
The heartbreaking beauty will remain
When there is no heart to break for it."

Afternoon light and heat on a day well over a hundred and you know the truth of it. Robinson Jeffers wrote of his beloved Pacific Ocean, but he spoke to the essential, heedless wildness of the world, the vast inhuman space before him most of his adult life; and this equally wild place speaks with similar voices, similarly inhuman, so I lose no sleep at all deflecting his poem to praise the space I know better than any ocean. Besides, he is dead and I am alive; his heart can no longer be broken, and mine still lives to praise the strange beauty in this desert space. I know, as did he, the beauty will endure long after there is any human mind to remember it. He and I will equally donate our constituent molecules to the air and water and life that survives us, but we will be far beyond knowing or caring. Our conscious life is so brief a gift, there are simply not enough waking hours to any one consciousness to understand so complex a miracle. There is barely enough time to master language sufficiently to attempt to praise what I see. How shall I praise, and why, the very gift that makes praise understandable? No, I simply give thanks, and move on to the more solid forms before me, the ones that mold and flow and distort only on a scale of millennia, eons, spans of hours so vast that I can safely call these cliffs solid and depend all my life on their support and shelter.

Still, I wish he sat across from me in this heat, that I had more than just his unalterable words to debate the greatness of the gift, the wonder of the stars, the simple sheer beauty of water. The remaining weeks would fly; the time of departure would simply be regretted as a human necessity for food and less essential companions.

What will I think of my civilization when I return? I have "terminated with extreme prejudice" a piece of its history, so I suspect I will find it somewhat more comfortable, knowing in my heart that I have the power to change it, at least a little, should I find that change worth the risk of my life. That will have to do.

I take the usual time and care to put the day's scratch on the wall. A nice long diagonal this day to complete my seventh group of five. Neatly blocked and orthogonal, I find myself now wishing I'd been more creative than the traditional patterns, but it serves well, is read easily as a reminder even in dusk, dawn, or moonlight. Day 35 is mine to use or lose, depending on the view. Looking back, after Day 3, the adrenaline was gone and the stately progression of summer days began. I can remember each day distinctly, each little flash of insight or remembrance, but the order shifts because the order is unimportant. Each day stands as a fragment of some older pacing to life: minutes, even hours needless, unless they impinged on survival. And my survival is now so easy, my demands on the space around me so few, that there really is time to see, each and every moment I'm awake. It seems like years since any such prior epiphany.

So now the gifts of time and place are freely offered: I have taken the time, albeit in a constricted space, but the real desert is out there, all around, undiminished, clearly visible. The real treasures require effort to assemble places and seasons and sunlight and weather, but having done this, the trick is to stop trying and just allow the simultaneity of mind and vision to create an image just so, have it fluoresce with its true and inner grace, so uniquely powerful that the mind will never fully recall it any other way.

So I have been here long enough. I have waited ever so carefully: not forever, but over a month now. And now, finally, I no longer preconceive what I see, but merely view what it actually is. That true image, of course, was always there, and no waiting was needed to bring it forth or make it visible. It has been there all my life, just as I see it now, but the waiting was for me. And now I am only here, no part of me elsewhere, no part of me hoping or dreaming or striving otherwise. Just me, just here, only now.

The beauty is breathtaking.

What I always wanted was always here.

It's good to be back.

VI

Horror comes with the night,
far in The Forest's heart
threats from all those others
unknown of face and number
between myself and home.

Fear from wanting life
to see the sunrise, be away.
Rifle slung, sidearm holstered,
knife in hand since noise means death.
Sweat of fear, humidity, heat
in huge green vastness
hiding an enemy
hiding myself

Blade become blood
slick and metallic
each one that falls
to hard skills, sweet luck:
more chances for life
no prize for second.

Feral steel ravager
savage survivor primeval
unleashed in the night
wants only to live.

Why are there so many?

Soft warm familiar pressure
slick against cold sweat
her loving touch the sunrise
"a dream beloved; you cannot die."

Understood. Half awake
suffused by joy
supposing it could be true........

Fully awake now: only me, still alone, still only here. It has been years since that dream of memory last replayed. She is not here to reassure me, but there is no sweat, and my pulse rests in the 60's. What does it all mean?

Can it be that the ancient rite of exorcism, the killing of the scapegoat, endured for so many centuries merely because it was true? I have forgotten no bloody detail, I even remember the fear, but I am no longer afraid. If that remains true, that alone will make all this worth the time and the risk. I would not have imagined so quiet a recalling, so calm a dreamed horror, knowing that those few I called beloved are all dead now, will never again be there for comfort in the dark.

And if, in my unimagined future, I should be so lucky as to honestly call yet another woman beloved, perhaps I'll not have to share the horror to make it endurable, having strangely made it no longer horrible.

Homicide as the giver of peace. I should have known it would be that easy. Given my surprise at how simple killing was thirty years ago, how pleasurable was the violent removal of a living threat after hours, days of tension, nights of sleepless fear. No church, no school in my youth had taught me that, had dared to express the sweetness of such uncivilized and forbidden fruit. It really was better than sex, and the schools and churches had lied about that, too. It would be the perfect circle, a most reasonable order to the universe, if the hauntings of those first killings that so tortured my soul should be erased by one last murder. I am not the storm to batter my enemy, nor the dream that brings peace for us both, nor the song of our humanity, a never-ending cry: only death. Falcon-like, I may have accepted my predatory, carnivorous nature, may now really know in my heart that killing to survive is what I am — no wrong or right, only life.

May it be so.

May it really be the last.

Day thirty-six, or so the wall says. And I have been careful with my morning ritual of engraving sandstone, each and every day, each day only once, only here.

I think of the more complex, thousand-year-old carvings, paintings, the petroglyphs and pictographs so hauntingly expressive under the overhang up canyon. I have always wondered why I find no sign of habitation in my little cave. It is wonderful shelter, and the Anasazi were never ones to waste good shelter.

Maybe it was good cover for ambushing deer and desert bighorn sheep in the wash bottom, and they left their celebratory praises for the place of cooking and eating, rather than the place of killing. Or more simply, maybe this place was under ground, below the sand of the wash bottom a thousand years ago. It is the ultimate human conceit to think the world is and was only as I see it.

Those petroglyphs show spears, bows and arrows, men dancing, odd and lengthy serpents, many deer and bighorn sheep. The pictographs are larger, darker, carefully drawn on paler stone walls to accentuate their darkness. Armless, imposing shadows four to five feet tall, still but not quiet, actually disturbing. It is hard to camp there, despite good shelter. Even in bad weather, I sleep better somewhere else, even if only a little way up or down canyon. I am not a superstitious man, but I have consistently sensed more than just shadows and stone there. I do them the honor of leaving them alone. They have owned the space for a thousand years; why should I disturb their rest? I leave them be. I detour to look at them every time I walk this canyon.

I look at the rifle: a little more dust, still undisturbed. I was never all that good a shot, even in my army days when there was lots of time and free ammo, and shooting was an honorable pursuit, good shooting a prized and highly praised skill. You weren't a gun nut, you were a dedicated professional, honing the skills that defined your life, then preserved it.

Yet there I was in March, this beautiful rifle sighted in at 400 yards, staring down at The River, staring at my rangefinder that said the opposite bank was some 540 yards away. But I'm shooting downwards, which will carry the shot a little farther, cause it to strike a little higher than would otherwise be the case. So, leaving the scope unadjusted, I laid the cross hairs ever so carefully on a piece of driftwood on the opposite bank, settled comfortably into a supported prone stance, listened to my slow breathing, then ignored it — only the target, only the rifle, any time at all.......

And the recoil was utterly surprising, scope image lost, ringing thunder rolling down the canyon, impossibly loud in the cool stillness. A covey of Chukar take flight upstream; a three-point buck flushes down canyon, bounds easily away. The silence returns, excepting the complaining decrescendo of the Canyon Wren, out there somewhere, where he belongs. Someday that lovely song will remind me mostly of death, instead of desert. Perhaps my efforts now will be the one to make it so. Reacquiring the scope image, I see a crater in the riverbank perhaps 8" low, but dead on line.

Scope adjusted a few clicks for elevation, a second shot is again on line, but 2" low. Another few clicks on the scope, and three straight shots hit the wood, grouping within 4". What a beautiful weapon! I have never shot that well in my life. But now the sharp focus of concentration seems so easy, relaxing into the shot, actually effortless. Could the thought of a living target now only of my own choosing make so great a difference? No orders from on high, no mercenary motive, no physical survival at risk: can the simple act of predation make these skills that much easier? I hoped so at the time; I know so now.

One magazine of five rounds, and I was basically sighted in on The River. This was going faster than I thought it would. I picked out a piece of wood floating down river, acquired it in the sight, guessed four miles per hour drift, converted that to six feet per second in my head, knew the bullet would take about half a second to get there from here at 2,800 feet per second, led the log some 3 to 4 feet, and fired. The geyser of water at the strike point was only off by some 6", so I adjusted my lead and took my other four shots, scoring hits on the driftwood with two. A happy man, I gathered up my brass and headed back up the side canyon.

I spent the rest of the day doing two more provision hauls down from the jeep five miles away. Then a late afternoon communing with the pictographs, pondering their former predatory selves. And a long, good night's sleep, the kind of sleep so easy for a body that has earned it. Months in the future lay the night I was earning to be mine alone.

Forty rounds and five days later, carefully altering times of day and number of shots, skipping one day due to river rafters, I knew I could dependably hit a drifting target a foot square five out of five times. Then I cleaned the rifle and hung it on the wall of my little solution hole cave to wait for July, to wait for one last shot.

I wandered that canyon just to explore it again, since I rarely came here in this season of late winter, early spring. As expected, the little details of the living were different, and the skies greyer, the winds harder, more sustained than the ones that stalked the summer's heat, the air I knew so well. This is, after all, some 4,000' above sea level. But the rocks still lived, still surprised me with their mass and vastness and infinitely varied little details of texture, color and fossils, fossils testifying endlessly to the ubiquitous, endless life force of the planet, wanting life, not caring much if it be human.

Sunrise and sunset slice up our lives frequently enough, it seems a shame to carry a watch here to slice it up further, butcher it thinner, taunt each pulsebeat with minutes, seconds, worse. I vow to leave it behind when I return, learn to lean on sunlight, moonlight, the stars — true and astronomical time. Here, far from the houses and highways of men, the simple communion of the days suffices, becomes more than enough.

It is good to take a few days like that now, since I will not have the luxury come summer, come the time when hunter becomes hunted. I will sit in my shade and think too much. But for now, all this rock and sky seem softer, more sensual, nearly verbal, as if my surrender of time had made me a friendlier receptor for their indeterminate powers, no longer hidden through the nights. Even the vast dome of stardust now seems approachable, touchable, every uncounted sun moving individually, each a singular plasmic dance, the huge whole a chorus of lights chanting visibly on an infinite stage, dancing to creation's silence.

I stare back until great chunks of the night shimmer perceptibly, outlines blurring to shapes unnameable, metamorphosing towards something else entirely, still unnumbered, ultimately so other than human that the sheer mystery of our peaceful coexistence becomes forever unknowable to mere mortals, myself, anyone at all. Yet still I continue to gaze upwards into the night sky, feeling utterly at home there, whether I deserve it or not.

What shall I do with the far insufficiency of mere language in the face of all this splendor? How shall I express the excellence I have found there, these beings of light with no color but clarity? Beyond my conscious permission, there seems no actual connection between my five senses and my civilization, and yet I still seek a private, recognizable taxonomy for what I have seen based solely on verbal metaphors for the spiritual consequences of this natural world.

I continue to hope for some superior insight, but I am persistently human, my errors consistently similar, far less interesting than the infinite variety of consequences.

VII

The light that dances high desert sunrise is the space's enduring muse. The truth will not be found in the words I can write of her, but it is among them.

When I was younger, I feared her only illusions, visions, hallucinatory dreamtime — but it is now thirty years later, and the images I see and remember are still the same, the struggle for the actual words just as humbling.

Noon in June a killer — merciless, indiscriminate, undeniable — light as heat only, heat to make us dream night, seek shade, worship water. Still and always the giver of life itself come springtime; the brilliant warm colors of autumn, even here; a simple, lovely hope in the brief clear days of winter. I cannot curse such hope and gifts just because the sun of summer kills.

I would like to become the same wild cold stone brightness when the wind is right and the days just so. The journey and great energy given willingly to become interstitial here forever — not that rock, or this sage, but always among them, along their every edge, like this air, like this remarkable light all around me.

But my energy, even great energy, has a biological price. Paying that price is, by definition, life-depleting — for me to live, something has to die. That price and this muse are rarely compatible.

Yet for a few hours there is only this light and the desert and me. And sometimes, only very briefly, there is no space at all between itself and myself, no boundaries whatsoever. I, too, am killer and light, coarse sands and cactus and great soaring stone, me and the muse; and the earth cannot have enough of her, for there are only we happy few.

The oval window that is the door of my cave, my view of the known world forty days and forty nights now, distorts, flows to different shapes, flickers to translucency, and the walls across the canyon merge to these walls so close, my space becomes claustrophobic, then huge, now small again, breathing light and space with myself seated in the windless air that nonetheless moves, throbs with life. Myself in the Desert's Heart......

I'm losing it!!!

But now, this one time, I kill the fear before it owns me. I'm losing it, yes, but now there is nothing to lose; so I let go. And so I lose it all.......

Summer sun, desert light: that which is not stone is light only. And I am stone, a sand cast of shapes long dead, coarsely granular, a molded reflection of wind and water and frost and millennia, mute testimony to the powers of weather and time and geology.

And I am the light, am light only, infinitely translucent, touching every surface, warmth for life, power for the chloroplasts, heat to kill the careless and unwary, make food for their betters.

My little cave is huge, is tiny, vast, flexible, pulses with time, pumping air and light and water, ceaselessly, to no purpose save itself, no reason that I need to know.

Adrift at last, actually timeless without being dead, fully alive to no purpose save the celebration of life itself. I got so much, and most sand got so little......surely I can accept such a gift?

I stop holding only myself and touch the walls, and the sandstone becomes solid, static once again. Only stone. Only home, shelter, defense from prying eyes. I shift positions, move to a different spot of the cave floor, frame sky in the window instead of desert, the act of motion both reassuring and frightening me that I and The Desert are separate, have not physically merged into a heartless singularity. I am happy to find only me.

I am getting to know this stone too well. And the minor degree of sensory deprivation in this small space is having its effects on my mind. Time distortion was first, but actually pleasurable: walking all 300 million of the years here at one time or another was/is an interesting temporal hopscotch, but this spatial distortion, this confusion of interfaces seems actually threatening, and yet so lovely in surrender. Logically impossible, but emotionally real is the fear of waking up half stone, or flaring and fading like dawnlight. Or is it only another gift I am offered? I never wanted to live as long as the one; never wished to become quite so evanescent as the other.

Our gift of flesh is so brief a memory, yet it speaks the truth, even here in the stones. The ultimate pulsation of life is still a heartbeat, second to second in blood-flooded darkness, briefly contained, testing the warm, wet, living limits every vital instant. Even unconsciously, my flesh tests those edges; but my consciousness utterly depends on those edges, leans its life against them every instant, trusting its every thought on their solidity. Dependably there, the assumption has worked well enough for fifty years: the dome of bone that overarches the only sky that matters exists forever unseen by the eyes that live there. Yet it speaks the truth.

The problem is not so much sensory deprivation as distraction deprivation — a very rare impoverishment of civilized senses. Here the inputs in the cool shade of summer stone are not distractions, but each and all actually meaningful, interpretable details of this very real world, this canyon's existence many millions of years prior to any mind with either capability or time to wonder about all these things here for what else they might be, the manifold aspects they most surely are.

And so I eat a little jerky, brew a little instant lemonade, savor each flavor and contrasting texture, wonder at this soft machine of life in the heart of all this stone. Only me, only human again.

Tell me again why I came back.

My friends and I, over the years, have debated endlessly about the spirit of place, especially the inspiring spirit of this desert. Selfishly, we continue to discuss it as The Desert, as if the vast arid spaces of North Africa or Central China were somehow meaningless, not germane at all to our wonderings about what brings us back here, especially in the killing heat of summer. But it really is like first love: this was the land that grabbed our hearts first. There are and have been other places, some of unsurpassed beauty, but there is only one first love. And I will wonder to my dying day why this was the first, why all this rock, this barely adorned surface of the earth, should attract the eye and the heart inescapably, unforgettably, as long as memory has meaning, as long as my little grey cells can talk to each other, all those invisible ionic dances in the dark I continue to recognize as self.

I'm not sure we ever agreed, even a little, about the actual, identifiable characteristics of that spirit, but I do remember we agreed on two things: you were much more likely to meet and recognize that spirit if you were alone with it, and it was not possible to consciously seek it out like some place or solid object you could acquire or possess. The very mercantile concept of possession became ludicrous before the kind of vastness and grandeur that came so easily to this desert, The Desert, the dream of sandstone and rivers that we never called ours. No, the power and beauty of those brief inhuman communions drove our lives outwards, out of our homes and into this desert, again and again, seeking, one more time, a brief touching with the planet's heart, the force that wants only life — not human life, not my life, but life itself, any and all equally valid, equally alive, similarly a moving feast of praise to The Desert.

And I have certainly been here alone longer than ever before, now that the presence of any other is actually a threat, only the life that lives here can be joined or even just observed without any baggage of risk or remembrance to distort the meeting. None of my friends or family even knows where I am. They think I'm up in the Canadian Rockies somewhere, hiking and climbing, having a grand time in a grand alpine space that I know well and have disappeared into many times before. My car is still up there, next to a trailhead, so why not?

If I do this right, no one will ever know I was here, nobody need share what I now know, the empowering secret that lives in my every imaginable future. I need not dilute it by speaking it to another like some mere boast of soldierly expertise, making it merely a kind of spiritual greed, rendering it an episode in some unexplainable linear nightmare conjured just to scare children, or politicians. And that is not the why of it, not even close. The power of the event I created is like unto the spirit of The Desert: you need to be alone in the knowledge, and you can't actually look for it. Oh, I looked for the event all right, but that was merely a physical performance, easily transmogrified by some stranger to this place and the event itself into some simplistic, movie version of conflict and vengeance. No, what it has done and become, here inside me, is so much greater than I imagined, than I could ever imagine, that I could not bear to lose it to braggadocio. I don't want to lose it in words; it is so much more than what the words might say, ever. And I didn't dilute the power of the event itself by sharing the effort, so there is certainly no point in trying to share it with another now via some superficial tale in words only. There is no understanding without being. I will not dream the strange and pointless dream of getting the words right, just right, now or ever. Either you were there or you were not. And I was alone that night, the only sharing with the air and the stone and the lone watchful eye of the moon. And when I walk out of here, get on with my life out there, then it will not be mine either. This alone is the time of power, when every day is a continuance of the one effort, when each day passed is an easy linear leap back to the night, the stillness, the single shot in the dark.

Clouds of stars lighting the night, gleaming endless galaxies empanelled on walls eternally black. All those stars endlessly adrift, fleeing away at unimaginable speeds, clearly seen by light millennia late, ancient photons oddly diluted by so vast a journey, mere fragments of an older, farther fury. Now only company for journeys, brief or endless, lights in the night speaking of planets unattainable, barely imagined, other lives in other places forever unknowable.

The God-shaped hole in the human heart, the one we call Allah, Buddha, Jehovah, Christ, depending on time and place, gestures compellingly in the night and aloneness, but I know much about sunrises to come, and I ask no other future. With my fingers I can touch the surface flesh, the warm, living interface between myself and all else, touching the walls of the one true prison, the one called human. Inescapable.

I am sometimes tempted, but understandably hesitant to purchase a Global Positioning System and return here, now measuring precisely the where of what I see. But the simple act of measurement takes time, and that time would forever be lost to the holding of the vision all around me, the mechanics of the numbers denying the magic that is here.

And should I carry such an instrument back to my Occasional Canyon, perhaps I could discover, once and for all, if so magical a location could actually be recorded on the maps of men. If it was there, of course. But assuming I find it once again, then I must return yet again some future date with my little numbers in hand to prove them reliably and repeatably true.

The hesitation comes with contemplating the extinction of yet another fragment of the ever-more-rare Terra Incognita, where longitude and latitude are measurable, but have no meaning, tell you nothing of the possibilities to be found there. As if actual magic could be measured, quantitated, had a number.

Neil Gaiman, British fellow, as I recall once said: "Science is a way of talking about the universe in words that bind it to a common reality. Magic is a way of talking to the universe in words that it cannot ignore. The two are rarely compatible." Which is close enough to the truth, even though at least half the magic I have experienced in my life is based entirely on science. The pure and simple truth of things is frequently miraculous enough for me. My internal contradictions go on, probably endlessly.

I would love to prove that Occasional Canyon actually isn't there all the time, that the precise coordinates of that location on the earth's surface still won't tell you what's there on any given day. Terra Incognita indeed.

Maybe the pervading sandstone here, even in brief human timescales, is more like the vast expanses of glacial ice: maps tell you it is there, but only being there tells you if it's snow or ice or the lethal, lovely blue depths of crevasse, the soaring pale towers of seracs. It is an area of high uncertainty, infinitely attractive for that little adrenaline edge to going there, living there in the actually unknown. Such a space seems more alive for its mutability, a place to be cautiously befriended rather than invaded.

Words ultimately have no meaning in such a place, as they cannot describe what will be found there, however detailed and exhaustively they may convey the surfaces you can see that day. Those who follow, or even they who return again to renew the acquaintances, can only come and see for themselves. Utterly unanticipable. There is no history but the personal individual memory. Any present recitation may easily be the last, certainly unrepeatable. Perhaps it is all the more valuable when no net of words can contain it, every conceivable biography inadequate, incomplete, ultimately useless.

I can tell you how, with perhaps a little difficulty, to reach the physical locale I now occupy. What you will see there is anybody's guess, any at all equally accurate, similarly possible, each of them Terra herself.

There is not enough simple magic in our day to day lives, confusing as we do numbers with knowledge, mere knowing with actual wisdom. I will bring no technology to my Occasional Canyon; time itself is threat enough. I will not risk the magic I have seen there to some soulless device that cares not at all, not ever. I will always mistrust the machine that guides nuclear missiles and lost children with the same effortless priority.

Hot air from so much rock remembering all that daylight far into the night, hissing sands in winds of arid heat spiralling skywards — only to cool so high, fall, be warmed anew by soaring walls of solar memory plated on stone. The cycle builds uninterrupted this night — higher, faster, ever-repeating, self-renewing — until charges unimagined are silent no longer, roar through the night, flare in canyoned silence and dark, banishing stars, night vision, sleep. Flickering fireworks of lightning welding air far up in the boiling dark of sky, the slowly echoing decrescendo of thunder cascading wildness across an already unimaginable landscape: real canyon, real sky, yet only a flash of strange vision, memory for a quieter future.

Now's my chance, only my second one in forty days. Out into the night, dancing barefoot in the warm sand of the wash bottom, swirling winds now warm, now cool: warm tasting of heated stone, cool smelling of water and sky. It's so good to walk and run and just jump to no purpose. I celebrate my invisibility from anything far above even as flashes of lightning make everything clearly visible, even me, but only here in the canyon, here where mine are the only human eyes, and all the others live here, are the canyon, are the desert itself.

The body was meant to be used. I have had enough of thinking, want only life, only thoughtless motion with the wind leading, dancing in the damp and the dark, loving the rain.

VIII

"You can't make the desert represent a freedom you should have organized for yourself in your bedroom or living room. That's what is so otiose about nearly all nature writing. People naturally shed their petty and inordinate grievances in the natural world, then resume them when the sheer novelty dissipates. We always destroy wilderness when we make it represent something else, because that something else can always fall out of fashion. Freedom to the all-terrain-vehicle addict, the mining and oil and timber companies, has always meant the absolute license to do as they wish, while 'heritage' is a word brought up by politicians to recall a virtue they can't quite remember. The only traceable heritage related to our use of the land is to exhaust it.

"When you first come to the desert, and I suspect it's true of any wild area, it's just a desert, an accretion of all the bits and pieces of information and opinion you've picked up along the way about deserts. Then you study and walk and camp in the desert for years, as we both have, and it becomes, as you say, heraldic, mysterious, stupefying, full of auras and ghosts, with the voices of those who lived there speaking from every petroglyph and pottery shard. At this point you must let the desert go back to being the desert or you'll gradually become quite blind to it. Of course, on a metaphoric level the desert is an unfathomably intricate prison, and you may understandably wish to play with this fact, comparing it to your own life. By not letting places be themselves we show our contempt for them. We bury them in sentiment, then suffocate them to death in one way or another. I can ruin both the desert and the Museum of Modern Art in New York by carrying to them an insufferable load of distinctions that disallows actually seeing the flora and fauna or the paintings. Children are usually better at finding mushrooms or arrowheads because they are either ignorant of or unwilling to carry the load."

Precisely so, Mr. Harrison. What The Desert really is cannot fall out of fashion because it will kill you if you are ignorant of it. If you cannot or will not learn its truth, your only alternatives are to leave quickly or destroy it. The burden of my civilization is that it has actually become easy to destroy, and so the rare conscious act of unselfish restraint is required for the space to ultimately survive our love of it. Or our terror.

I have heard often enough over the years the geologic labels for every layer of ancient sediment In these canyon walls, but I am happy to say I am still not quite sure which is Navajo and which is Coconino sandstone, although the presence of the White Rim sandstone is so obvious that the label is inescapable. Sort of like my struggle with Occasional Canyon. But I don't want accurate knowledge of these labels to fool me into thinking I know what I see, rather than making the effort to see it change daily with light and weather and seasons, no label sufficient to encompass its even daily variety, not to mention the realization of its self as swamp bottom, mud bank, beach for the basking dinosaur.

The names of these canyons, this River, the layers of stone exist only on maps, in books. We name them so we do not lose our way. We name them so as to avoid the struggle for accurate description each and every time we wish to speak of them. Such a struggle would cause one either to not speak of them at all or to know them so well that the description would be effortless. Either alternative seems preferable to the misleading ease of labels. Probably we name them because we are lost already. Why else do we wander so? The Desert knows, has always known which canyon has water, which has jasper, which meanders like a maze. The Desert knows, and cannot lose them, just as The Desert itself cannot be lost. Nothing awaits it; it wonders not at all. Each day in this desert is made of what has come before, only here even geologic pasts are so easily visible that we think the future, too, must be known to it. But each canyon will be as surprised by the next day as myself, though they will accept its shape and textures more easily than I imagine.

No, I am the prison, not this desert. The walls are human, not stone, and it is both the gift and the blindness of my education and intelligence that is the real struggle. It is an effort to simply let my curiosity run free in the space itself, and only later wonder about what it actually found there.

Like the storm of five (or was it six? A glance at the wall and its scratches, all 45 of them. OK, five) nights ago, when I ran up-canyon to see the pictographs by lightning light, flickering under the overhang, sometimes soft in the shadows, sometimes leaping out in rare direct light when a bolt of lightning would flare low enough to the rim behind me. Magic. But not The Desert. At home here, but not really of it. Images of travellers like myself, living here long time or short time, but just passing through, the human parade at the surfaces just too brief a presence to register on stone. These few painted pleas to a stormy night are seen by me, have meaning to me, but not the storm or the stone. Their creators are in that place that The Desert has chosen for them. They are where they are supposed to be, though I have no idea if they chose also. No far fossil future can contain them, only a little darker dust to drift the wash bottom, someday launch off the jump-off become briefly waterfall, thundering in some distant storm I'll not live to see.

I chose to be here. I know I am where I want to be. That is a bit of good fortune to sleep with all the rest of my life.

I walked down canyon, now downstream in 18" of flash flood, to see those very falls, hear and feel the roar of that drop resonating in its ages-old amphitheater of its own creation. Thirty years of walking and floating the Green River, and I had never seen those falls when they were actually falls. There in the night, the vision I would most likely never see again danced and roared and misted the shadows far below. Brief lightning flashes lit the scene, showing in stroboscopic unreality the power that carved the space.

Two canoes and two tents on a sandbar on The River. Ah yes, still the season of effortless floating on this river without rapids. Still more evidence that the culture I came from exists even now in recognizable form. Something out there to go back to, should I so choose. Probably their first trip, and from where they are, they can only see the top hundred feet of the drop. I couldn't believe they weren't hiking up this side canyon just to witness the display of simple power. But I never saw them outside their tents. You don't hide from summer rain in the desert, you dance in it. Oh well, don't have to worry much about them hiking up canyon to where I hide. Drift on, tourists!

Gracefully undulant, pale silk of waters binding forever these desert canyons to a far mountain heart; sandstone and granite, the unshared geologies miraculously coexistent, sharing now this selfsame River: one Source, the other Result, each carried inexorably away, just so, by the endless soft strength of water and gravity to the identical ocean, the same roar of thunderheads flaring in the summer's nights, brief penumbral revelations of a future unwitnessed and judgeless.

A wonderful night. A couple of hours of walking around and getting rained on. Been awhile since the last bath, and it sure felt good. Something about skin loving water; some instinct for the sea of our species birthing, or just some more recent image of warm amniotic floating in the dark? Regardless, in desert summer, water is precious, rain is magic, a bath away from the river a priceless gift. And I had it all in one hour. Luck beyond belief. I'll take it.

Dry and hot ever since. 45 days makes it late August now. I can actually start thinking about leaving. Arbitrarily, I have chosen the next rain after day fifty for my retreat. Rain to erase all evidence of my passage, though wet stone will make the ledge traverse and climb down that avoids the jump-off real interesting. No matter. Such concerns seem trivial so far away from the first few days of real risk, that brief time when I knew without looking that the powers that be wanted me badly. I mean, discharging a firearm in a National Park is bad enough, but aiming it at someone and actually killing them probably had the Park Service and the Utah State authorities arguing over jurisdiction — just the sort of bureaucratic stupidity I was counting on to make my life easier while I was here, and long after I leave. I'll try not to mention camping two months without a permit to anyone important. And I'll be careful running The River out of here, since I don't have a permit for that, either. Wouldn't do to get ticketed for that with no ID on me and myself supposedly in Alberta. Things to do yet.

Ah yes, trivia to contemplate while carefully carving groove number 46 in my wall. This kind of still heat could build up an impressive thunderstorm any day now; one little nudge from a southern jetstream, the local monsoon flow, and the collision will be impressive. Go ahead, think about leaving: a couple of days of River, a couple of days of Lake Powell ("Lake"! Disgusting reservoir, thinly disguised cess pool is more like it. Merciless killer of Clearwater Canyon, the Cathedral in the Desert, and other drowned wonders too numerous to mention. Give me a SADM charge and I'll blow the Glen Canyon Dam tomorrow and not care about dying afterwards, after so great an act of mercy) and a long hitchhike from Hite to Montana, a veritable stroll over the Canadian border to my car in the wilderness (where did I hide that distributor rotor?) reconnect the battery cables, fire that sucker up and head home. Plenty to do in the near future to get from here to there. Things to do.

Ah yes, Day 46 of the same food I chose to live with, survive on months ago. I'm not picky, but I seem to have chosen well. I have beef and turkey jerky, and small 3 oz. cans of bacon bits for protein and salt, and over six weeks later, the variety of flavor is not boring. For carbohydrates, I have assorted cereals: bulky, but not heavy, so easily carried in, far back in an early spring, barely remembered now. And the cereals I chose carefully are fortified with assorted vitamins and minerals, just to be safe for so long a stay. The dried apples and other fruit leather, as well as some hard candies, add a little sweet to the days. I really do miss chocolate, but this heat makes that not possible. So it goes. Still, I look forward to the choosing of my meals. But would I love a little fresh fruit and vegetable, a glass of cold milk, ice cream, other pleasurable gastronomic indulgences of my distant past! Ah well, at least I have instant lemonade to kill the increasingly plastic flavor of the water in my bottles. That water is still the only thing that makes life possible here in the summer , when warmth is not a problem, is often the enemy.

But I can see now I have plenty, have eaten less in my inactivity than I thought. I usually eat a little more when still and bored, a fact I frequently noted in the long nights of winter camping out in the far snows, but while very still indeed, I have only rarely been bored. Bless The Desert and all its infinite variety! Maybe there's a good reason why Moses, Jesus of Nazareth, Mohammed were all prophets from the desert spaces. The Wisdom of The Desert, through their words, has powered my civilization for millennia. Far future history will no doubt someday judge if that was a good thing or not; for now, it is all I have: that and The Desert itself. Some of what I see here is different.

The little flashflood of five nights ago washed away some of the seed pods from my local Datura, even now preparing to bloom once again, squandering more water. So those seeds are down canyon somewhere, hunting for soil and sunlight to call their own Good hunting!

I hope my little migration down canyon will work out well. If I get through all this, I wonder what I will grow into, what light and space and food will seem somehow suitable after this effort? What will I grow into after all this nurturing in The Desert? I hope my journey here speaks less of the truth of history and more of the truths of men. Not some solitary man exceptional in his hatred, but closer to the reality of most humans than my civilization cares to believe or admit. I hope I will recognize what I have become. I hope I can learn to live with it back in the houses and highways of men.

The enmity of my world was a surprise to me thirty years ago. Cold and unyielding, dependable as sunrise, I am surprised no longer. Now I am part of the hardness in the heart of the world, no longer having any cause save myself to stand against it.

I can close my eyes, regardless of the daylight, and still dream the moonlit night I created near here. I can be again the death that waited, remember the surprise of the day before when my target stopped to camp on the sandbar and I realized I would not have to shoot a moving target, however sedate its drift downstream, recall the shock at such outrageous good luck, as if the target chose me also, made it easy in a final empathic gesture. But the details of the dream are not so vivid, even this soon after. It is hard to count the fossil tracks in the stone across canyon in the moonlight. It is hard to recall the colors of the tents, the raft. Only his head, haloed by silver hair in the moonlight, stands out, each detail as sharp as ever.

Doubtless as the memory of that night slowly fades, so must it fade in my dreams, the loss of detail in the dream merely evidence of the loss of the memory itself. Even now I wonder if the empty places hide more than they ever revealed when I could see them, remember well.

And the rifle on the wall of my little cave: some days its simple mechanical metaphor for American inventiveness and craftsmanship is a kind of power, the power of life and death it so typically represents in Western myth. The superficial characteristics of that image forever unconcerned with the more subtle and delicate power of decision: the long, very personal debate that can be action can be also stillness, the rifle rightly only the solid, touchable representation of the immaterial act of choosing. And some days it is only submission: a giving over of my more humane and delicate self to the training of thirty years and unnumbered wars ago, a simple surrender to an old shame and an older pride in lethal skills wielded well. The blood in us all paints the difference. Red is for power.

All this is not a matter of illusion, not my simple jest in past lives at reality being a crutch for people with insufficient imagination to dream well, but a thought that all remembered details merely serve to keep this desert at bay, this true and unimaginably ancient desert. The light I see at the stone and the living surfaces is a thin membrane only; the real power, the forces of motion and solidity, are all deep down in the darkness that is the truth of the planet's heart, and no man lives or wanders there. Endless blackness reflecting perhaps only the true and natural condition of the universe, all that space before and after our stars, these few billion years of light merely a brief celebration of the secret core of darkness at the timeless heart of eternity, time itself meaningless without the passage of the stars to mark its minutes. Blackness beyond imagining. Nature does not reside in what I can see, or even what I dream I saw.

My words, my thoughts, speak in a darkness only briefly commensurate with the motives of a living planet. The prior and latter silences will testify to the more usual disproportion of life and death.

Thoughts about death bring me inevitably back to Mary's death, a passage far more significant than anything I have done or seen here this year. Certainly she had no death but her own to apologize for, and I could not accept apology for so simple and reasonable a choice to depart this life on her own terms. We had discussed it at length over the years — the medical professions we practiced so long stimulate that sort of conversation almost daily — but that was mostly intellectual abstraction. I was more proud of her than I could ever tell her the day she made her own choice about the how and the way of death. She did not surrender to the cancer that was going to kill her slow. She fought when there was a chance for success, and those battles bought her many good years, but she was smart enough and brave enough not to fight again when the metastases reared their numerous and ugly heads, knowing as we did that those tumors could now eat chemotherapy for breakfast. The choice was hers, and she had the guts to make it: to enjoy her last few months, instead of struggle and vomit in the grips of near-fatal doses of assorted toxins. She did not "go gentle into that good night" but instead walked away easily in the home that was hers and in the arms of the one who loved her above all others.

It was an easy choice only on that last day. The morphine that it took to control the pain was so fogging her consciousness that even I realized the gift of the body was gift no longer. While it was still all of her that I could hold, while all that she considered self was still there to hold me back, she asked for the last thing I could ever give her. In her honor, I could do no less. At the time of her choosing, I gave that last injection into her intravenous line, and we talked of the actual times and places shared that were now only photographs on our bedroom wall. Each image remembered well, each odor and season and sunlight — all those things we knew that the photographs did not — each lived again briefly in the words and gentle silent touches shared those last few minutes. Even her final smiling jest about who else her age could I spank on her birthday. I got to watch the light behind those eyes I loved so well fade irretrievably, and I will hear her last soft sigh of breathing echo through my future far louder than any gunfire in the dark.

I like to think it was the breathtaking beauty of one of those real places and shared days, and not the many milligrams of morphine, that actually took her breath away.

I felt so good about her choice, so at peace with the way of her departure, that it was days later before, selfishly, I could cry for my loss and the irreplaceable hole in my future.

I donated her ashes to the silt of the Green River in this very Canyon three years ago, thinking then I would never return. Instead, yet another death at my own hands brings me back, one final but intimately lengthy journey. And I wish a quiet, slow death in the arms of a friend for myself, and not a final, curious flash of light, off to my left, halfway up a cliff, way out in the dark.

I wonder which future waits for me. Will I have friends good enough when my time comes to use the needle, or only enemies good enough with guns?

That man and the Government he stood for was energy enough. They squandered my generation's belief in the United States for nothing. And then the survivors from my generation told their children all about it. Now hardly anyone believes. Mostly, we are not Americans anymore, but stockholders in U.S., Inc. We neither want, ask for, nor elect leaders anymore, but managers, cops, and accountants, more or less honest. We got what we fought for. I am angry because it is not what I was told I was fighting for. But I learned. I am no longer a hired assassin for the Government; I will choose my own targets, thank you.

IX

Long and lovely dreamtime
sleeping the dreams of stones
breathing starlight and dawn
becoming impossible airs
clear and arid and huge
each itself only.

Sufficiently withdrawn, consciously not recalling, no emotions filtering or distorting the true information all around me. Not quite human for a little while, no heartfelt humanity for insulation to deny me the reality of this space I have labored so hard to join — that same endlessly inhuman, unsurpassingly lovely, merciless desert space I wish I actually understood, dream to live, sleep to dream.

Too many days, however joined or separated by years, of a shared but uncommon language — wordless, fiercely objective, awash with sunlight, the sounds of flowing blood and the smell of no water at all — barely, only briefly decipherable, utterly devoid of metaphor, but language nonetheless.

Listen, and I will show you a truth unremembered, actually forgotten — or I would not be here to tell it.

Day 49, and fitful breezes interrupt the usual stillness of morning. The feel of air just a touch more humid than usual bespeaks the possibility of interesting weather this day. A glance out the opening to the sky, and the presence of a few clouds so early promises a different day entirely for The Desert.If the storms come, maybe I should leave today — a logistically trivial decision, since I need take nothing with me. Everything I need for a week is buried on the other side of the river, directly across from the killing ground, the one place they would have no cause to search. Maybe today I get to find out.

I wonder in retrospect if this place of my choosing is an area where the acts of man and the acts of The Desert are similar, perhaps of the same piece. Probably not; I buried what little was left of my wife here, but it was ashes only, useless to coyote and vulture and catfish. And it is sweepstake odds that the corpse I created on a sandbar seven weeks ago is not buried here. No sound of full military honors have I heard in this space. No, we the people are persistently human, even in death. Secretly, we have no wish to return to our origins, but wish instead to transcend such things. No matter, such things will come and take us by force someday: a perfection quite unimaginable, not at all human, waits for us all. But not long.

Between our actions and our ceremonies are the real storms and stones: one to build the whole world with, one to tear it down, a sand grain at a time. The huge process of the planet itself is utterly careless of our comings and goings, and this is the earth we do not see. We see the bridges over the canyons and rivers, the dams that make lakes out of the rivers, the seawalls that hold back the sea. All these things last many years, maybe even centuries, and we of so brief a life are much impressed. The geologic ages that are the life of our planet will little notice nor long remember what we were or why we came. We may, of course, leave interesting fossils, though we have no real wish to contemplate what minds will come in the far future to wonder at our leavings.

I hope we the humans, the hairless apes with the oversized brains, will ultimately evolve to be that future consciousness. Magical molecules of DNA, deep in our every cell the helix that remembers, may also tell our future. Selfishly, I wish for beings with a little introspection, a far distant memory of what we are now as a heeded warning, a path finally recoiled from so that the future, in some small way, might be us, know a little of what we were and cared for, remember us. But I have my doubts. It will be too close to call from here.

Far future children,
birthed on planets as yet undreamed,
your genes the only reminders
of a far and forgotten earth,
when you orbit our galaxy's final star,
call the Milky Way your own,
and gaze at unexplored vastness beyond,
remember we also dared things beyond our knowing,
we also have known beauty.

And if you could see what I have seen these last few weeks, you would never have left. No, sadly, it is the few who are literally blind to the self-regenerative beauty right here who will finally find a way to leave. It will not be me. My galaxy is the sands and stones right here. It is enough.

And this time, when I leave, I really won't come back, ever. Like the rifle, to return would be to dilute the purposes for which I came. In my mind, it is a formed space. I will bring too much emotion back to any future float of the Green River to ever do it justice, ever again see it only for what it is, instead of the stage I made it for selfish and too-human acts. When I finally divorce the actions so carefully performed here, I will do them the honor to leave them alone, to vanish unremembered, here in The Desert, as all things living surely do.

Overall, what I really want is for my small, soft feral self to live what it feels, be only what it sees, do only the dictates of hard, wild necessity. And some few days here I have actually done just that.

It is with eyes thus empowered that I can see life down beyond the microscopic level all around me, within me here. At some transitional molecular level, all life becomes at least imaginary, even inconceivable. Life there is so different from our day to day lives it approaches, then becomes abstract, barely graspable as discrete entity, reproduceable, intelligent, conscious. But life nonetheless. Life so critical, that none of us would be alive to discuss it were it not so at the heart of all living, or even pre-vital matter.

Outside, in the sand here, the juniper, the jimson weed, the cacti, all those very desert plants with root systems far larger than the visible green that eats sunlight and breathes: at the root, tactile, pheromonal level their lives speak, each to the other, far beyond our imagining, much greater than mere photosynthesis, moisture, reproduction — those things we have studied, know fairly well. The vast web of the living land they dance so slowly in, struggle with, help create speaks back to them all in illogical but needful terms, ceaselessly, in words not heard or even perceived as language. But that is what I hear, even now. Ultimately, all our lives on earth depend on it, and for fifty years, I sensed it not at all.

Like two people deeply and lengthily in love, knowing in their hearts too well the third entity they have created that is only themselves together, but so far exceeds the sensible sum of their two lives that it is almost laughable to tell even a good friend what they are talking about when they say only "we", I have no way to verbalize the simultaneous indescribable beauty and astonishment I have found at the planet's heart, at the edges of these rocks, the roots of those plants, and my simple act of being here, surrendered to their time and so privy to their inescapable dialogue. I have always been a part of that, but I never knew it. I wish I could remember what I haven't heard all those years until now. Dreams lost.

No conscious thought needed
The soft perfection of your body
Lives regardless, labors to be so
Entirely without your permission.
Let it be and it will let you wander.
Let your mind wonder
And the wonders of this earth
The sea of sky and the swimmers of light
Offer themselves to your senses.
You are free to create your life entire.
You cannot know how long that takes.

Mental exhilaration that has consumed half the day, and yet I have so few words to tell of it, to even hint at the miraculous all around me, nonverbal but undeniable. Now the afternoon dark clouds and cool winds tell of changes, demand attention. Up from the vast order of a grain of sand, a fragment of lichen, and out into the huge chaos of sky and great weather. There is a world out there, more vast than I have remembered in a long time. Time to go back, perhaps. Time to have time matter, once again. Time to be motion, action, linear series of events to become recognizable history, amenable to mere words. Things to do.

The weather continues to build, dark clouds show curtains of rain evaporating halfway to earth, but the sun is still high and driving all this. There is much more to come. But now I am shielded from the sky, and only an idiot with a death wish would fly a plane below this building storm. Thus concealed from the human aspect of the skies, I drag my sewage container out a final time: old 30mm cannon ammo box, it has served me well and handles easily, since I got to bury its contents only nine days ago in the last storm. It's not hard to find another tree that will appreciate the wealth of nutrients herein, but I search out a place where I can dig deep and away from the wash bottom. About halfway to the jump-off, I find yet another perfect spot and it is easily done this last time in 15 minutes.

The wind gusts down the canyon, episodically stirring up blinding clouds of sand, Dust Devils to dance for the stones, an orrery of sand grains to spin its brief sketch in the air, showing the stones in the ground what the stars in the sky have in mind for them, for me, for us all. I leave the ammo box and shovel in the wash bottom and hustle back up to my cave. A final glance at the contents: I stuff my sleeping pad and blanket into my rucksack and grab one bladder of water. I will leave the remaining water and food to some other needful soul. The small waterproof ammo can contains over 200 rounds of match ammo, but the rifle that goes with them stays here, and so do they. I give a final reverent salute to the rifle hanging from the climbing bolt in the wall: now it begins to long outlive me here. Fare thee well, companion in the wilderness; I could not have done this without your excellence, the skills of craftsmen far away.

It is hard not to simply stand partway up this sandstone wall and just peer into my unlikely home these past two months. The view in seems so foreign to the one outward I have lived with so long. Therein are my few concrete tokens to this canyon: the rifle the power to destroy, the food and water the power to let live, and my four books the powers to grow in spirit, to grow where it really matters. Those four books: each protected in its doubled plastic sealable bags, scratched and dusty but serviceable, abandoned but well remembered, read and reread, extensively underlined, earmarked and otherwise skewed to my personal perceptions. Small extensions of the profligate powers of their creators, a few of their gifts handed down, carried on, still living within me as faithful companions for the too-long nights in spaces of steel and glass and all those others.

And deep and neatly patterned, 49 grooves in the wall of stone. This is all I leave that might possibly be seen by eyes other than my own. The millions of flakes of dead skin cells from my very living surfaces are no doubt everywhere, and microscopic mites and bacteria will doubtless feed well here far into the future, but that is yet another world, not mine or my kin. The sewage container down canyon I will vanish with me, the only token that tells I am only human, not spirit, malevolent or benevolent. Let some far future first finder decide. I know.

Now become relic, it is past and history, and I lose myself to the spirit of the breaking storm as I walk down canyon, loving the thunder and the cool and the first drops of rain. The folding shovel goes in the rucksack, and I carry the old ammo box down canyon to the jump-off. Clouds of wind riffle The River, moving upstream at varying speeds, hissing through the tamarisk, still promising serious rain, but mostly noise and bluster so far. The canyon below the jump-off is empty and no one camps on the sandbars yet this afternoon. Nevertheless, I wait and watch a little, enjoying the crescendo of the weather, becoming more sure that I am alone here.

A large pool of reddish, silty water remains below the dropoff, remnant of storms prior hiding in the endless shade of this amphitheater. Keeping it simple, I simply drop the large ammo box off the edge and watch it fall some six or seven seconds to splash down with an impressive echoing crash. So lightened, I walk along the edge to the small seep that has been there every time I have, thus sufficiently eternal for the likes of me. Its few ounces per minute of endless rainfall tail off into the distance of the drop, disappearing into the swirls of wind, landing anywhere at all.

Desert seep of water so rare here, away from The River, purely antipodal to all this lifeless sandstone; water here so exceptional as to be only and absolutely itself, utterly unambiguous. Days, or mere hours of summer without such vital partaking and there can be no poetry, no truth, no art save survival. But having tasted, there can be life.

Dark, wet, sculpted stone shining with seep water, this flowing, banded wall reflects back a distorted, darker image of all that it sees, all that is visible. Deep in this canyon's heart, I see the shadowed space all stone, the undulant sky and light of life far above, and also a darker self twinned in this moisture's mirror, some orphaned essence, small fragment of ancestral me born of water long ago, to water now returned, windowed away here forever, this selfsame slash of skylight eternally aglow, all these rocks forever immutable.

Such mirror has doubtless seen all passages here: hunter and prey, curious explorers, lost aboriginal, careless wildlife, the dead and the dying rushing by in flashflood. My pale and wandering self is easily accommodated, barely remarkable. Here now is that merely visual representative of the fragment of my heart that wandered here, loved it, never left.

And I, origin of the fragment that sought the space, willingly offered it days, weeks of my life and was not refused, I leave it lovingly, neither my coming nor my going mistaken, knowing I could not stay and live, remain human; knowing in my heart I will not return, surrendering to the magic of water and geology that overfills my heart, obliterates all voids where fragments once were born, nurtured, and wandered away.

Drink now — on my knees, face to face, lips caressing this simplest molecular god, the true giver of life. There is only my antiphonal systole, my one heart for distraction, for praise. All else is wind and sand and desert. Only time, the fire in which I burn, consumes also these.

I squint up canyon into wind and sand, unable at the last to decide if I am leaving home or heading home. It is an honest transition from long waiting to long journey, and the myriad distractions of making progress, logging the miles, will delay any real deciding. I leave, regardless.

On to the ledge traverse, a sudden transition from roomy wash bottom to narrow ledge, with three hundred feet of rock wall rising from my right hand, and three hundred feet of air and gravity in my left. But the ledge leads directly to the huge talus slope, and soon it's only thirty feet of air and a fairly easy climb down to earth and sand and rocks. I'm halfway down the slope when the sky explodes, a wall of pelting rain roars over the rim, fogs the canyon, soaking everything in mere seconds. That stops me. I will get to see my falls in daylight after all, and I am certainly not stupid enough to head down to the bottom of the canyon now, grab the ammo box, and die in the flash flood that surely will come. I'll wait, thanks.

Dimly, across The River, I can see myriad waterfalls of varying size already launching off the canyon rim, sometimes cascading across the sediment lines, sometimes vanishing in the winds, carried away, added to the rain below. Now a few small rivulets fall from the edge of the jump-off, but these are mere local runoff: the side canyon is gathering force as the storm moves up canyon. It's only about five minutes, but in the midst of all the wonderful wet alterations to the space around me it seems much longer. Too much happening, as usual in such storms; I try to look everywhere at once and keep losing track of what's behind me. I can even look down at my feet and see the little orange and green-grey lichens brighten, intensify, swell in the sudden life-giving moisture they sometimes wait months to feel.

I can hear and feel the flood some thirty seconds before a three foot wall of wood, small stones, and muddy brown water launches off the rim of the jump-off, fans out, accelerates downward, whitening with air, a crescendo roar that ends with a reverberating huge slap at the bottom, explodes in all directions as mud and spray. The pool at the bottom rapidly fills, swirls and undulates and launches off towards The River. My large ammo can/sewage container bumps a few walls with odd, out of place metallic clanking, and rumbles off downstream. Ah well, one less thing to carry. Wonder where I'll find it later?

The roar of the falls now grown steady fills the space, can literally be felt as a subsonic pulsation in the chest wall, making the sound subconsciously ominous, even though I know it's no threat to me up here. Regardless of logic, it adds an edge to the display of raw power, gravity and water awesomely entwined, up to their usual efforts, sculpting the planet's surface. Too bad if you're in the way.

The rain stops abruptly, as the storm moves rapidly westward. A patch of sunlight reflects blindingly off the wet canyon walls up river, then vanishes, following the storm. The falls taper off rapidly, become a mere trickle in a matter of ten or fifteen minutes. Wonderful display! Thanks for the sendoff. My thanks, of course, falling on no ears at all, but still my almost reflex human response to grand and priceless gifts.

Mud in the wash a minor hassle as I work my way downstream, so as I clear the cliffs, I climb up out of the wash and parallel the base of the cliffs, smelling the little touches of wet juniper here, the magic, quintessentially western desert odor of wet sage there. Under a small overhang is an intact Anasazi stone storage grainary, the wood and mud mortar that seal the cracks still intact a thousand years after its construction, preserved by the aridity of the desert itself and the sheltering stone sky its builders chose so well. No other evidence of an entire civilization's passage is visible here, mere centuries later. A vanished race. The Disappeared People. I look around at 1200' canyon walls, sky above, River and plant life below, a lone Great Blue Heron gliding effortlessly upstream: these are the place. Few or many, I and my kind are just passing through.

On to The River's edge, the surface now littered with leaves and twigs and wooden debris washed off the rims, down the side canyons: more flotsam to help fill the reservoir far downstream. I swim across to the sandbar in mid-river and walk upstream on wet, firm sand. It is larger than two months ago, so I can only approximate the standing point of my victim. There is, of course, no trace at all, no evidence that it was ever more than the dream I live with. Rightfully so.

I gaze back up at the rim of the jump-off: 540 yards line of sight, as I recall. Somewhere up there, in a small dark hole well up a slickrock wall, sits the only evidence I was ever here, ever there. One lone thunderstorm, and I am not even a memory here. Rightfully so.

I walk to the far side of the bar and enter the river, the water seemingly warm as it stops the rapid evaporative cooling of the desert air. I drift easily downstream, swimming only a little, letting The River carry me to the rock slab on river left that lets me get through the wall of willow and tamarisk that makes most of the riverbank impenetrable. Then over to a few more large rocks and take off the rucksack, unfold the shovel, and dig up my gear. I put enough ground pepper in the sand all around here so even if they brought in dogs and even if they brought them here, it wouldn't help much. They didn't, it seems, and my cache is undisturbed.

It takes only half an hour to blow up the inflatable kayak and rig it down by the river. Still no sign of other river runners, even with a two mile view upstream. I wait another thirty minutes: no sign of slow leaks in the boat. My luck continues. I eat a little candy and nuts, and launch into the current, myself now part of the effortless downstream progression of the canyon's heart.

I am reminded of Oroborus: the snake eating its own tail, ancient mythical symbol of endless, eternal cycles. This River; all that sky. The River flows forever because the sky brings the rains, the snows, dependably, millennia beyond imagining. This same River, that same sky, ageless in all the ways that really matter, mine now by the simple gifts of time and effort and pure luck.

A couple of hours later, I drift by the mouth of Water Canyon. A group of people with two rafts and two kayaks is camped on the huge sandbar downstream. They are at one of the premier sunset display views in the canyon, and I hope they will be as wondrously surprised by the show as I first was some thirty years ago. I am tempted to stop and see if I can still talk to strangers after two months of isolation, but I wonder what I look like with two month's of beard, and I am in no mood for questions and certainly have no wish to be memorable here. A friendly wave from the far side of The River suffices to make me just another. And there on the sandbar they probably have no idea how magical is the perennial seep and swimming hole only half a mile up canyon. Wonderful place! Even John Wesley Powell, the first recorder of histories to float this River, floated by this side canyon unawares. Far be it from me to tell mere strangers otherwise.

Two hours later, I arrive at The Confluence, the junction of the Green and Colorado Rivers. This used to be where The Grand River began (hence the "Grand Canyon", downstream from here), but some mapmakers changed their minds, and ours; so from here to the Gulf of Baja, the Colorado River is The Source.

Upstream, back there, my little cave lies forever hidden, perennially perdue, a rifle its inert steel palladium, the ignorance of mapmakers and the sloth of tourists its only sure defenses.

X

I leave what I was those years ago at that auspicious location, the previous origin of grandness itself. There, where the Green River blends with the darker silt of the Colorado and vanishes forever, nameless, I should leave the man who is only dream now, a small memory in the sweep of years, the huge spaces of before and after.

I continue to assume the entire process was predominantly accidental, since the sequence of coincidences that made it all possible is so absurd that dream is the best place for the memory. Regardless, that man no longer exists. Once again. And I feel that, although brief, it was a wondrous existence, however the consciousness of it may have come to be.

For that little while, where I was going was of no importance, since where I was more than sufficed — the earth unadorned, a fine and private place, out there. It and I paused together, just long enough for my interiors to match the spaces, a little. What I have seen and understood in here, inside myself, has endured far longer than my presence in so huge, magnificent, and inhuman a place, out there.

There is no risk, no way of becoming lost when the whereabouts of everything else is of no importance, takes on true significance, if only for a little while. There, where I was, was enough.

So now, out here, adrift in the night, looking back long and well in the fine fog of nonexistence, I can hope that all I gave, so long and so hard, to all those fine places was sufficiently synchronous to that time and that space only that it went entirely unnoticed, is not remembered at all, even today.

I alone am the fire that remembers.

All those days become then only the good, solid, dependably there bridge, sure and certain transport from time past — what I was and what I knew — to my future life and my self to be. I built no house there, left discoverable but no visible signs of my passage, my presence past. Later now, deep in that future, I can look back and see only the bridge, the span of days across the space and time where no one dwells, not for long, not ever. The place thus remains, even in my memory, only the place, the magnificently sculpted ruins of a buried and dessicated swamp with no living referents, no conscious mind that knows nor remembers.

Sorrow at such a parting is meaningless.

A Week later, far away, headed still further north on a bus in Montana, I took advantage of so transient and anonymous a space to speak at some length with a few of my fellow travellers about what I had "missed" over my weeks so far from the houses and highways of men. What had the summer done that I needed to know? Not much. I even inquired specifically about the rumored passing of a past Secretary of Defense. Not one of my brief companions headed elsewhere knew what I was talking about. Just so.

Well done. The future will be only itself.

I who have been hunter will not be prey.

XI

Upstream, deep in the canyonlands where the maps say Land of Standing Rocks, in all those changing shadows the man who did these things got lost. More importantly, he stayed lost.

It is hard to envision that vast sandstone desert as a purely chrysalisine space, my full fifty years prior only some larval phase, growing towards something totally unimaginable by the larva itself — unanticipable alterations befitting any true metamorphosis. Yet that is all my memory sees.

Regardless, it is good to be something new, launched on a final(?) phase of unknown duration. Back there, still upstream but now much farther, the lovely stone chrysalis I left behind no doubt still hangs on the cliffs and the sky, unrecognizable to any save myself, the only one who actually knows what he grew into and became there.

A rifle still gathers desert dusts on the walls of some sandstone egg; bags of water warm and cool, day and night, tasting more and more like the bags themselves; books and words, protected in plastic, perfectly still, lovingly left, lying unread; a small metal box still cradles, protects all those well-crafted cylinders of brass and powder that make magic, extend the power of life and death to merely human hands.

The Desert remains immiscible, utterly incapable of joining with anything not already itself.

It is only a memory.

I have never returned.

The Canyon grows old:
Even rock is not forever.
The River ever older:
Eternity was never water.
Time makes myths of all things endless.
I shall drift away from this clear desert space, these soaring sandstone
    cathedrals, the roof of stars, this daily flowing celebration, the unattainable
    air.
My culture of concrete and steel reabsorbs me entire, welcomes me back.
Life quickens to undecipherable speeds.
But each day in the desert is my armor: my memory serves me well.
Whatever future comes, I will know all my life that the universe pauses.
I have been there and seen it happen.

Afterword

"Their mother drove east through thickening phantoms

And is thought to have died of thirst in the desert,

Or have killed herself,

Because she was hunted like the last wolf

And never found.

Her car was found overturned in a desert gully

Off an abandoned road;

That was perhaps the place where the phantoms caught her;

The wolf-hunt failed.

I cannot tell;

I think she had too much energy to die.

I think that a fierce unsubdued core

Lives in the high rock in the heart of the continent,

Affronting the bounties of civilization and Christ,

Troublesome, contemptuous, archaic

With thunderstorm hair and snowline eyes

Waiting...

- Robinson Jeffers -

"Solstice"

1935